TALES OF WHIMSY,
VERSES OF WOE

poems by
Tim DeRoche

drawings by
Daniel González

REDTAIL PRESS

REDTAIL PRESS

Published by Redtail Press
Los Angeles, California
www.redtailpress.com

Library of Congress Cataloging-in-Publication Data in

progress

DeRoche, Tim

ISBN 978-0-9992776-1-4 (hardcover)

Fiction

Book layout, design and illustrations by Daniel González

Printed in the United States of America

First edition

1 2 3 4 5 6 7 8 9 0

For Neve, Orik, and Solomon
– T.D.

For my niece and nephews,
Isabel, José, and Alex
– D.G.

Comprehensive Inventory of Gloom and Glee

If your moral character is flimsy
Or your wit be rather slow,
Oh dare not read these tales of whimsy
For often do they end in woe.

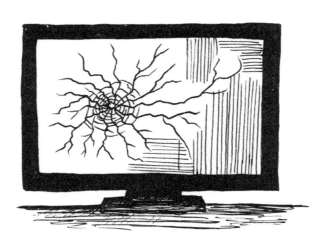

Mary Melissa Miranda McGurk

Mary Melissa Miranda McGurk

Was uncommonly fond of homework.

Nothing whatever could bring her more glee

Than mapping out battles from French history.

After each spelling test, she'd ask, "When's the next?"

Before jumping into some dusty old text.

And the easiest way to incur Mary's wrath?

Just switch on TV while she worked at her math.

Soon Mary noticed that to study and figure

Only made her head grow thicker and bigger.

This pleased our young scholar immensely

And spurred her to labor ever more intensely.

At first the enlargement was steady and slow,

And everyone cheered as they watched her head grow.

But then she set out to read *War and Peace*,

Which caused the rate of expansion to increase.

Pretty soon Mary's head was a bit too wide

To fit through the doorway to get outside.

Her misshapen head was darn near full

Of arcane information—quite unusable:

Asian capitals and historical dates,

The official flowers of all fifty states,

The locations of stars, the names of popes,

And the chemical makeup of dishwashing soaps.

Alas! Our Mary then felt a pain in her mind,

And a crack in her skull the doctor did find.

Two hours later—oh, her fate was the worst!—

Mary picked up a book and her head simply burst.

All over the walls were pieces of brain,

And blood fell from above like a midsummer rain.

So next time your mom says, "Please do your homework,"

Remind her what happened to poor Mary McGurk.

The King of the Land

The King of the Land
Had a band.
They practiced their punk,
But they stunk.
"That noise is too loud!"
Cried the crowd.
And so they did fling
The crown of that King.

Carrot Talk

Mr. Banana, a sensitive fellow,
Took offense when the Carrot called him yellow.
Mr. Spinach thought the Carrot mean,
When the Carrot called him "young and green."
But Miss Pepper was insulted not,
When the Carrot remarked, "Oh my, you're hot."

Miles and Leagues

Miles and leagues and more miles did I run,
Each day trying vainly to outrace the sun.
Flying west through the day, that star never ceased
To disappear nightly, then rise in the east.

"Oh, why do you flee me?" I cried to the sky,
But that arrogant orb made not a reply.
"Perhaps I can help," came a voice from behind.
"Hear me, my friend, I was once of your kind.

"In pursuit of the moon many years did I waste.
Month after month I kept up the chase.
And month after tedious month did I cry
As the crescent grew thin, then vacated the sky.

"Until, that is, I gave up my pursuit
In lieu of a venture that yields more fruit.
Wanting a job that would generate coin,
I opened a hardware store out in Des Moines."

Considering the man's kindly advice—
And my own lifelong aversion to mice—
I enrolled in classes to become an exterminator,
Then opened a small shop just north of Decatur.

Sleep Through the Night

"Sleep through the night
Without fright!"
I yelled heartily
Out of glee
To the townspeople all
In the hall.
"The Monster of Dread
Is now dead;
And Sir Lancelot slew
The Goblin of Rue.
So raise up your voice
And rejoice!
The Reign-of-No-Fun
Is now done."

The Boy on the Hill

The boy on the hill
Grew a gill.
"Why, that is absurd!"
Said the bird.
"Of use might it be
In the sea,
But you haven't a prayer
In the air."
So the boy with the gill
Left his hill,
Ran down to the bay,
And swam away.

The Story of Salmon Delicious

There was never a fish so ambitious
As the one they called Salmon Delicious.
"If I must be eaten," he told a friend,
"In the mouth of the King will I meet my end."

So Salmon swam all around on the look
For a royal worm on a golden hook.
Oh, many a year did he search for that bait,
Until an elder turkle set him straight:

"Go to the beach twenty miles to the east.
There does the King cast for his feast.
But be forewarned, you aspiring young fish,
As they say, you just might get what you wish."

Ignoring the chelonian warning,
Salmon swam east that very morning.
And when he arrived to bite on that line,
He read with a tear the words on the sign:

"A coup has overturned the monarchy;
The serfs have set up a democracy.
The dead King they are a-buryin',
And the new President is a raving vegetarian."

Salmon hung his head at the thought of his fate.
Never would he sit on the royal plate;
Never would he bathe in the richest of sauces
As the main course for the boss of all bosses.

But his sadness quickly turned to laughter.
"I'll not forget this lesson from hereafter:
I'll be a fish of the people—and not a traitor—
When I'm devoured by a legislator."

The Beast in the Cave

The beast in the cave
Didn't shave.
His beard grew in size
Up o'er his eyes,
And his whiskers grew down
To the ground.
He cried, "Woe is me …
I can't see!"
On a stone he did trip
And he tipped,
Falling down with a bump
On his rump.
Forever after there he sat,
Hairy, happy, and increasingly fat.

A Good Morning

Each morning I wake up a bit too grumpy,
Because a pillow filled with gravel is too bumpy.
And my bathroom faucet cannot make me clean,
Since it only brings me lukewarm gasoline.
I brush my teeth with superglue,
And wash my face—oh yes I do—
With leftover soup I find in the trash
(Which leaves my skin with a nasty rash).

So if you see me on the way to school
And you think I look like an ornery mule,
Perhaps you are inclined to scoff
Or to scream with fear and then run off.
But if you ask me, "How are you?"
I do reply—oh yes I do—
"Thank you, I'm quite well today.
How was your morning? Are you okay?"

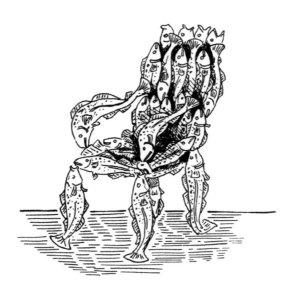

A Rope Made of Soap

A rope made of soap is too slimy,
And a muffin made of dirt is too grimy.
A marshmallow car might be squishy,
But surely a chair built of cod would be fishy.
But then, taking this even further yet,
Would a door made of juice be too wet?
And what about a pond filled with Dalmatian puppies?
Would it still have room for full-grown guppies?
I suppose it's silly to consider
An ancient castle made of kitty litter.
But I can't help but wonder,
What sound is made by meatloaf thunder?

Ugggh …

These incongruous thoughts have brought me pain,
So now I'll rest my bicycle brain.

'Twas for You

'Twas for you that I butchered the beautiful beast,
And for you that I dueled with Sir Andrew the Least.
For you did he fight me with anger so keen,
So for you did I swallow the magical bean.
And now 'tis you who must suffer in kind,
And helplessly watch as I go out of my mind.

Mudshakes by Mikey

Step right up!
Come one, come all.
Grab a cup
Of the Original.

We've got Mikey's Mudshakes here for sale,
Made by the famous Mikey Moran,
Professor of Mud at the College of Yale,
Formerly Shaker for the King of Japan.

Step right up!
Hear my call:
Just ten bucks
And that is all.

Imported mud from the south of Peru,
Mixed with a teaspoon of hollandaise sauce
And a dash of our secret ingredient, too,
Known only to Mikey, since he's the boss.

Step right up!
Come one, come all.
There's quite enough
For all y'all.

Out of seventeen doctors, nineteen agree
That our special mudshakes cause the flu,
And just you think how lonely you'll be
When everyone's sick except for you.

So step right up!
Come one, come all.
Grab a cup
Of mudshake tall.

The Road Well Traveled

I took the road more traveled by,
And though the path was often dense,
I'm thankful that I was not shy,
For pilgrims many happened by,
And to me their wisdom did dispense.

Home Above the Range

Oh, give me a sky
Where the buffalo fly,
Where the deer and the antelope soar.
Where seldom is heard the song of a bird,
Because the air's filled with ungulates galore.

The Great Philosopher

"Ignore the forest for the trees,"
Thus spoke Calamaties.
"And do unto others,
As they do to their mothers.
Sleep not for lack of trust,
And mingle only when ye must.
For life is but a slice of pie
That's eaten by some other guy."

CALAMATIES

Daddy, Oh Daddy!

"Daddy, oh Daddy!
A monster, I fear
Is here in my room
Hiding ever so near."

"Do not worry, my son,"
Said my Daddy to me,
"For a thing like a monster
I surely don't see."

Out came the monster from under the bed.
It growled, it snarled, then bit off Dad's head.

"Mommy, oh Mommy!
Please come to my room,
For a hideous witch
Just rode in on a broom."

"Don't be silly, my son,"
Said Mom at my door,
"For witches aren't real,
Only figments of lore."

Then the witch did appear as if out of a fog,
And suddenly Mom was no more than a frog.

"Granny, oh Granny!
 Come save me from death,
 For a dragon is here
 With fire in his breath."

"Now, Timmy," Granny said,
 As my forehead she kissed,
"Dragons aren't real,
 They don't even exist."

In through the window the dragon did fly.
In a breathful of fire poor Granny did fry.

"No more monsters!" I yelled
In a desperate tone.
"Get out of my house—
Leave our family alone!"

But out of the closet a goblin did jump
And swallowed me whole with a satisfied "GLUMP!"

I Like the Girl

I like the girl, and she likes me,
But all I feel is misery.
So just you think how much worse it would be,
If I liked her, and she didn't like me.
Or if she liked me, but I was turned into a tree
By an evil wizard named Merlin McGee.
Oh, how horrible that would be!

Jabber-Not

'Twas not brillig, and thus no slithy toves
Did gyre and gimble in the wabe.
Not quite mimsy were the borogoves
And nary a mome rath even tried to outgrabe.

So we—the Jabberwock and I—
Decided to end our senseless strife.
I took him home for apple pie
And introduced him to my wife.

Slubber-slop! And smicker-smack!
I only got a crumb.
The goolicious pie he did attack,
Leaving us quite hunger-glum.

'Twas not brillig, and thus no slithy toves
Did gyre and gimble in the wabe.
Not quite mimsy were the borogoves
And nary a mome rath even tried to outgrabe.

The One-Man Band

While I can make all kinds of noise,
It's 'specially fun to burp.
And when I've got some extra time,
I also like to slurp.

Sneezing, too, is quite a sound
And glorious fun to boot.
But farting is my favorite noise:
There's nothing like a toot.

Not for Naught

Not for naught did I scale the great wall of cheese,
But in vain did I swim the river of peas.
Not for naught have I trained this rabbit of yore,
But in vain has he suffered the rigors of war.
Not for naught was I born with one extra toe,
But in vain have I tried one more finger to grow.

NOTE TO READER:
Not for naught did I struggle these rhymes to dispense,
But in vain were my efforts to have them make sense.

Beyond the Gate

At the Gate, there stood a man
Who wore a uniform of gray.
A stack of papers in his hand,
He asked me, "Will you pass this way?"

I replied to him, "Oh, kindly guard,
I do so wish this way to go.
For though the way be long and hard,
What is Beyond I wish to know."

"Ah!" said he, "Beyond the Gate ...
A land of countless wonders rare.
Pilgrims many hope and wait
To pass by me and wander there.

"But I must follow protocol,
And all the rules that are the norm.
Go take a seat out in the hall
And please complete this standard form."

But I was not inclined to wait,
So toward the Gate I made a run.
Sliding past the guard and through the Gate,
I found myself in—Burlington.

Oh what a place of beauty fair!
With everything I'd ever want!
I did resolve right then and there
That never would I leave Vermont.

The Contraption

Oh, what a contraption! What a machine!
I drop in a legume and out comes a Bean.
In goes a femur and out pops a Bone.
It makes something Bigger after it's grown.
But the Best thing of all—you'll surely agree—
Is when I tried the amazing machine on me.
It really did such an incredible job,
For I started as Robert, but now I'm called Bob.

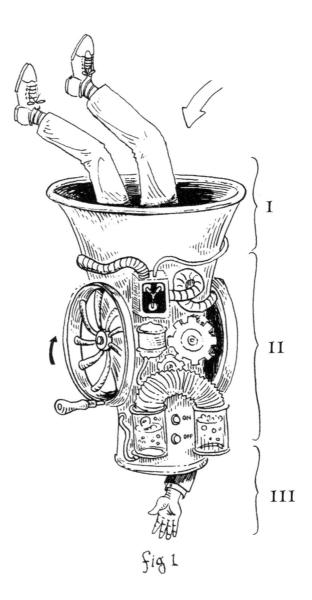

I

II

III

fig 1

Family Rock

My mother drives a hot rod car;
Her Christian name is Millie.
She prefers a Fender for guitar
When she riffs that rockabilly.

Now Daddy is the rhymin' guy;
We call him Master Pap.
Hip-hop is his chosen game.
Man, can that dude rap!

The biggest in my family
Is my older brother, Doogie.
He plays piano gamely,
And likes that boogie-woogie.

Over there at the computer
Sits my sister, Monica.
Live music doesn't suit her;
She produces electronica.

And my parents made a big mistake
When they named my brother Cisco.
'Cause hustle lessons he did take
And now he loves that disco.

Me? I'm the youngest in the kin,
And they aptly named me Wyatt.
I just can't think with all this din …

I WANT SOME PEACE AND QUIET!

Mystery Poem

Oh, when did she do it?
And what did she do?
For whom did she do it?
And which of us knew?

Where did he hide it?
And how was it hid?
From whom did he hide it,
Wherever he did?

Why did she say it?
And how could she say?
To whom did she say it?
Was there a delay?

They certainly knew it.
I know it was true,
For I saw them do it.
And I did it, too.

The Bear in the Boat

The bear in the boat
Couldn't float.
His body weight
Was too great,
And he started to sink
In a wink.
"My plight were less grim
Could I swim,"
He growled with a frown,
Going down.
But he grabbed the tail
Of a whale,
Who gave him a hand
To the land.
That night in his bed,
The Bear said:
"No longer I'll wait
To lose weight.
From now on no meat
Will I eat,
And I'll spend less of my hard-earned money
On honey."

Bailey O'Bannon

Bailey O'Bannon hated all that was green.
"Of that color I am not so keen,"
She told her parents in a fit of rage,
Using words inappropriate for one of her age.

"I must rid the world of that heinous hue,
For I am partial to red and to blue."
So off to the local store did she run.
A doubt in her mind? There was none.

"Give me red and blue paint—every can in the store!"
She yelled at the clerk, as if going to war.
"Why so much?" he asked her politely,
Not knowing the subject wasn't taken so lightly.

Said Bailey: "So green will no longer exist.
So that color will simply cease and desist.
Emeralds, grass, and Ireland, too—
All will look better in red and in blue."

"What a worthwhile plan!" exclaimed the young clerk.
"Would you grant me the honor of aiding your work?"
Eager for help, Bailey nodded okay,
And thus the conspirators went on their way.

At her house they unloaded the gallons of paint,
And Bailey spoke up with a major complaint,
"Oh!" she cried, "you are such a dumb fellow.
Instead of red paint, you loaded the yellow."

"I'm sorry for such a stupid mistake,"
Said he: "But amends, I promise, I can make.
When your parents call you home to bed,
I'll stay alone and paint in your stead.

"To paint all the Land we have enough blue,
And the cover of darkness will hide what I do.
You go inside and sleep well through the night,
And all will be covered before morning light."

Bailey gave him her blessing and went to her room,
Excitedly thinking 'bout green and its doom.
She said to herself, "I can't wait for the dawn,
For then every trace of that hue will be gone!"

She woke in the morning at first ray of sun,
Out of bed, down the stairs, to the door did she run,
Eager to see the results of her plan
And wishing to thank the helpful young man.

With a turn of the wrist, she opened the door
And—in shock—fell with a thump to the floor.
She saw that all of her plans were now dead:
The world wasn't blue—but all green instead!

The houses, the sidewalk, the birds in the trees...
Seeing this sight brought the girl to her knees.
All the cars, her bike, and the thick morning fog—
All of them greener than a Tanzanian tree frog.

She followed the paint tracks to her very own school,
Thinking, "I must find that color-blind fool!"
By the dumpster she found him, green head to heel,
Humming and painting an old orange peel.

"This is not the world of which I dreamed!
What's going on here?!" Bailey screamed.
Looking up from his work, the clerk snorted with glee
And simply replied, "I confess it was me.

"You picked the wrong clerk for your ill-fated scheme,
For I harbored an equally difficult dream.
The color green is what I love and adore …

... So it is green that shall reign in the Land evermore."